The Incredibly Special Balloon

Marguerita J Rainbow

Balboa Press books may be ordered through booksellers or by contacting:

Balboa Press
A Division of Hay House
1663 Liberty Drive
Bloomington, IN 47403
www.balboapress.com
1 (877) 407-4847

ISBN: 978-1-9822-1988-8 (sc)
978-1-9822-1987-1 (e)

Library of Congress Control Number: 2019900405

Print information available on the last page.

Balboa Press rev. date: 01/23/2019

BALBOA
PRESS
A DIVISION OF HAY HOUSE

Bella and Beau are baby angels who had almost become little beings, long ago, but changed their minds, just in time. They didn't want to leave their friends, or Angels Playschool. They even forgot about the special balloon.

Bella and Beau love to play in Cloud Land after play-school. They especially love to look through their doughnut cloud into the world beneath the clouds.

One afternoon a big red balloon floated up through their special cloud.

"Hey look," said Bella, "it says I LOVE YOU. And there's a note tied to it."

"Cool," said Beau. "I wonder who it's for."

"Me too," said Bella. "I wonder who it's from."

"What if we go in to the other world to find out?" said Beau.

"How?" said Bella.

"We could slide down a rainbow," said Beau.

"But Mr Love says we have to wait to be born to go to the world beneath the clouds," said Bella.

Mr Love was their teacher at Angels Playschool.

"Yes, I know," said Beau, "but it would be fun, and we can find out who sent the balloon."

"OK ..." said Bella. "I've always wanted to slide down a rainbow."

And so it was decided. They would find who sent the balloon and tell them it arrived.

Bella and Beau loved an adventure, and one was about to begin.

The baby angels quietly tip toed through the fluffy clouds until they came to a giant multi-coloured slide reaching all the way down to the other world.

"Hey look Bella," said Beau, "we found it! Are you ready? Quick, take my hand."

They jumped onto the rainbow.

"Wow," Beau screamed as they took off, "this is fun Bella!"

They hurtled through all the colours of the rainbow – red, orange, yellow, green, blue, purple and violet – all the way down the rainbow into the other world.

When they reached the end they jumped off and looked around. It seemed very strange and different to Cloud Land.

There were lots of people everywhere, there were cars and bikes and mummies and daddies. Kids playing and lots of strange hairy creatures.

There was so much to see, but they had to find who sent the balloon.

They saw a boy on a bike. "Let's ask him," Beau said. He hurried up to him and politely asked, "Do you know who sent the big red balloon to Cloud Land?"

But he didn't take any notice. He just rode right past.

"Mr Love said that not everybody in the other world believes in angels," Bella said. "I don't think he can see us."

"Ok," said Beau, "let's find someone who can see us."

They went from one person to another, but no one could see or hear Bella or Beau.

"What are we going to do?" asked Bella. "If they can't see angels, we can't ask them."

The baby angels were beginning to wonder if they had made a mistake, when they heard a voice say, "I can see angels." Bella and Beau couldn't see where it came from. "Over here." Bella and Beau looked behind a tree. "Not there silly, I'm up here." The baby angels looked up and saw a little girl sitting up on a branch.

"Can you see us?" asked Bella.

"Yep," said the little girl. "I always see angels, they are my friends."

"Cool," said Beau. "Do you know who sent the I LOVE YOU balloon to Cloud Land?"

The little girl thought for a minute. "I don't, but I know someone who might. Let's talk to the Lollipop Lady, she knows everyone."

She jumped off the branch and leaped onto a skateboard. "Jump on!"

Bella and Beau hopped on and wrapped their arms around the little girl's legs, and she took off.

"Wow, this is awesome," said Beau as they whizzed through the busy streets.

They stopped where a lady with a giant red lollipop was blowing her whistle to stop the cars.

"What's she doing?" asked Bella.

"She's helping the kids cross the road," said the little girl.

When the children were safely across the little girl went up to the lady. Bella and Beau followed, a bit dizzy from their fun skateboard ride.

"Hello," said the little girl. "Have you seen anyone sending up a big red I LOVE YOU balloon into the clouds?"

"As a matter of fact I have," said the Lollipop Lady. "Just this morning I saw Lucy letting go a big red love-heart balloon in the park."

The baby angels were excited. "Thank you, thank you," Beau yelled, even though the lady couldn't hear him, and he rushed off up the street to find Lucy.

"But Beau, we don't know where she lives," Bella called out as she ran to catch up to him.

Beau stopped. "I didn't think of that."

They looked back to where the Lollipop Lady and the little girl were, but they were gone.

STOP

"I've got an idea!" said Beau. "Let's find the place where they make balloons. They will know."

They walked and walked through the winding streets. They were too young to fly. Their small legs were getting very tired, but they had to keep going. They couldn't give up now, it was their dream to find the person who sent the big red I love you balloon to Cloud Land. So they continued on, until finally, up ahead they saw a sign: Balloon Factory.

"Hey," said Beau, "that's it."

They ran as fast as they could to the door.

Inside, they couldn't believe their little eyes. Stacks and stacks of balloons everywhere. And the red I LOVE YOU balloons, shaped like a heart. Hundreds of them all tied together.

They rushed over to the counter to ask the man standing there.

"Do you know who sent an I LOVE YOU balloon up to Cloud Land, with a message tied to a piece of string?" said Beau.

But the man couldn't see him. So Beau climbed up onto the counter and asked again.

"Do you know who sent an I LOVE YOU balloon up to Cloud Land with a message tied to a piece of string?"

The man turned around, picked up a cloth and wiped the whole counter, almost knocking Beau onto the floor.

"Nobody can see us," said Bella, feeling a little scared. "We're never going to find Lucy and we're never going to find our way home."

The baby angels stared at the balloons. Ideas were running out.

All of a sudden one of the I LOVE YOU balloons broke away from the rest and floated out the door.

"It's a sign!" said Beau. "Quick, let's follow it."

Reluctantly, Bella trailed behind Beau, who was chasing the balloon down street after street.

It finally turned another corner and came to a halt. Bella and Beau turned the corner just in time to see a little girl grab it. She looked surprised.

The little angels stared at her holding the big red balloon.

"Do you think she can see us?" whispered Beau.

"I don't know," Bella replied.

"Hello," said the girl. "Where did you two come from?"

"She can see us!" Beau said.

"Of course I can see you," said the girl, still holding the big red balloon. "My name is Lucy. What are your names?"

The baby angels looked at each other in shock. "Bella and Beau," they replied.

"Did you send an I LOVE YOU balloon to Cloud Land?" Beau asked.

Now Lucy looked shocked. "How do you know that?"

"Because we saw it float up through the hole in our cloud," Beau said.

"We wanted to tell you it arrived," Bella added.

Lucy stared at the baby angels and her eyes filled with tears.

"Thank you," she said. "You've made me so happy. It's my birthday today and this is the best present ever."

"What does it mean to send an I LOVE YOU balloon to Cloud Land?" Bella asked.

Lucy looked at the balloon she had captured. "It's very special," she said. "My daddy went home to another world and I was so sad. Then one day my nannie gave me a balloon and told me to send it up to my daddy, with a little message from me. So I wrote I LOVE YOU and tied it on to the balloon with a piece of string. I went to a special place where Daddy and I had lots fun together and let it go. I stood and watched it float up into the sky until it disappeared. And you know what Bella and Beau?"

The little angels shook their heads, eager to hear the answer.

"I didn't feel as sad any more. Because I realised I can send him a special balloon with a note just from me whenever I want to. I can write anything I want to tell him.

"And since then I always send up an I LOVE YOU balloon every birthday and Christmas. It's very special. I never forget."

"I'm glad you're not as sad anymore," said Bella.

"Thank you," said Lucy. "I want you to take this balloon back with you. It will look after you on your journey home."

Suddenly the baby angels remembered that they didn't know how to get back to Cloud Land. Dark clouds were forming above them and lightning flashed across the sky. The little angels wondered if Mr Love had discovered they were missing.

This was scary for Bella and Beau.

"How do we get back to Cloud Land?" they asked Lucy.

"Don't be scared, I know a secret that can help you find your way home. If you make a picture in your mind of Angels Playschool, all your friends, your teacher, and all the games you play, and keep thinking of that picture, over and over, it could help to move the clouds apart."

Bella and Beau were trembling. The thought of being stuck in another world as baby angels was frightening. So they tried very hard to imagine being back in Angels Playschool with all their friends and Mr Love. It felt so real they believed they were back in Cloud Land.

Surprisingly, the dark clouds opened up and there was the rainbow. "Come on!" Lucy called. "Follow me. We have to find the end of the rainbow, before it disappears."

They ran as fast as they could and found the end of the rainbow. "Hurry," said Lucy, "run through the colours to the other side. There you will find the moving stairs that will take you back to Cloud Land."

They rushed through each of the seven colours and the stairs appeared. It was time to leave.

"Goodbye," called Lucy. "I'll never forget you Bella and Beau."

They waved goodbye and jumped on to the stairs, which started to move, slowly at first, then faster and faster.

Up up up they went, through the rumbling thunder, flashing lightning and wind shaking the moving stairs. It was scary for the little angels.

They held on tight to the special balloon, as they travelled back up the other side of the rainbow.

"Hey Bella," Beau shouted, "I think we are almost home."

"I know," said Bella, "I can see where the rainbow begins."

"Awesome," Beau said, "I think we are almost back in Cloud Land."

The sun had almost disappeared and the moon glowed softly on the two little angels.

They quickly jumped off the rainbow before it vanished.

They hurried back to their special cloud, still carrying the big red I LOVE YOU balloon.

"Hey look Beau," said Bella as they got closer. "Something else is coming through the hole in our cloud."

As the baby angels watched, a brightly coloured balloon popped through the hole in the special cloud and floated right up to them.

Bella was still holding the I LOVE YOU balloon. Beau grabbed the other balloon.

"Wow", said Beau. "It's from Lucy."

"What does it say?" asked Bella.

Beau looked at the balloon.

"Thank you."

Printed in the United States
By Bookmasters